Sojourner Truth's
STEP-STOMP
STRIDE

Andrea Davis Pinkney & Brian Pinkney

Disney • JUMP AT THE SUN BOOKS
New York

She was big. She was black. She was so beautiful.
Her name was Sojourner. Truth be told, she was meant
for great things. Meant for speaking. Meant for preaching.
Meant for teaching the truth about freedom.
Big. Black. Beautiful. True. That was Sojourner.

Sojourner was born a slave. Her master named her Isabella. Sojourner's mother, Mau-Mau Bett, and her father, James Baumfree, took a first look at their child and decided to call her Belle. Seems her newborn's cry was ringing in good news. Nothing quiet about that girl.

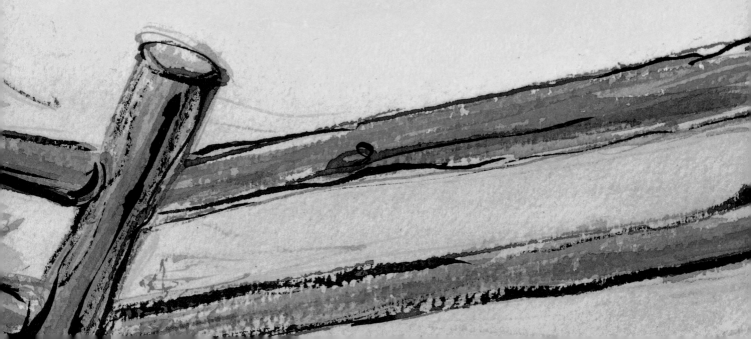

Belle grew quickly. She was almost six feet tall while still
a child. Along with her size-twelve feet, she had hands like
hams. Lots of muscle on her bones, too. And no one dared
pick a bone with Belle. She could plow, hoist, and haul
better than any child her age. With her big-soled shoes, she
could stomp the beetles that tried to eat her master's corn.

Belle's strength and size made her valuable. She was sold away from her parents when she was nine years old, and to two more masters after that.

This was the ugly way of slavery. Belle hated being treated as property. And she hated shucking, boiling, hauling, and working all day for her master, John Dumont.

John Dumont knew how strong and capable Belle was.
He promised to free her if she worked extra hard for him.
Belle wanted her freedom more than anything. So she
stepped to it. She worked hard for many years. She polished
Dumont's brass until it gleamed. She mucked his horse
stalls. She churned the Dumont family butter twice as fast.

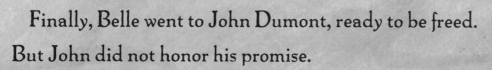

Finally, Belle went to John Dumont, ready to be freed.
But John did not honor his promise.

That's when Belle decided to run away.

In search of freedom, Belle ran. She fled like tomorrow wasn't ever gonna come. She covered some ground, child. She got *gone*.

She refused to stop until she saw hope.

Belle ran right up to hope's front door. She came to a farm owned by a Quaker couple, Isaac and Maria Van Wagener. The Quakers were abolitionists. They believed in freedom for all people. Isaac and Maria offered Belle shelter.

When Belle's master, John Dumont, caught up with her, Isaac offered to buy Belle's services. It wasn't Belle's work that he wanted—he wanted to free her. Belle's master took the money from Isaac, then *he* got gone. Right then, Isaac freed Belle! And even though Belle didn't have to run anymore, she set out on her own.

Belle went to New York City, where she could be truly free. And, oh, was that freedom ever *sweet*. Freedom made Belle want to take the heels of her size-twelves and kick them up high. Belle celebrated her freedom by marching her feet straight to a job.

Belle worked as a maid. A maid who *made* money for the work she did. No more master. No more cotton to bale, beetles to stomp, or corn to shuck.

Belle soon learned that to celebrate freedom, she had to speak her beliefs. For her, freedom meant helping others. Freedom meant putting her foot down for what she knew was right. Freedom meant she would "travel up and down the land" to share her ideas. That's when Belle changed her name. She gave her slave name the boot, and called herself Sojourner Truth. She said the name Sojourner was just right for someone who was a traveler. And Truth—well, that was what Sojourner did best—she told it like it was.

Sojourner couldn't read or write. But she could sure speak her mind. And now she was free to go wherever she wanted to find folks who could help spread the word about freedom. She met many abolitionists, women and men who spoke out against slavery.

In her travels, Sojourner made a friend named Olive Gilbert. Olive was an abolitionist. She read the Bible to Sojourner. Sojourner memorized every word in that good book. She could recite the entire Bible — from the "begats" to the Beatitudes.

Sojourner told Olive all about her childhood as a slave. Olive wrote down Sojourner's story. In 1850, *The Narrative of Sojourner Truth: A Northern Slave* was published.

Sojourner carried her book with her everywhere. She spoke about the unfair treatment of black people and women. When Sojourner preached, she let her words fly. Free as the highest dove in the sky. Free as the sky itself.

Sojourner's voice was packed with power. As she traveled, she learned even more about the meaning of freedom. She found that freedom is not a place. Freedom is the fire that burns inside. And Sojourner Truth, she was full of fire. Once, when Sojourner was scheduled to speak at a rally, someone threatened to burn down the building. That didn't stop Sojourner. She said, "I will speak upon its ashes."

In 1851, Sojourner step-stomped to a women's rights convention in a church in Akron, Ohio. There was no rain on the day of that convention, child. But, oh, was there *thunder*. What struck that spot was strong and loud. It was Sojourner's step-stomp stride.

There weren't any big, black, beautiful preachers in that church. Yet the main question was, *Should women have the same rights as men?*

And you can bet the men at the meeting had something to say about *that*. Most of the men were ministers. Like Sojourner, they knew all the words in the Bible. And, same as Sojourner, these men were following their own strides.

One minister said that men should have "superior rights and privileges" because men were smarter than women.

The next man to speak said that men should be allowed to boss women around because Jesus had been a man, and that God wanted men to rule the world.

Then came two more speakers. The first one opened his Bible and said that women were lower than men because in the Garden of Eden, Eve had given in to the serpent and had eaten the apple of temptation.

This minister's friend said that women were too weak to deserve equal rights because they needed men to hold open doors for them, help them into carriages and over puddles.

Well, that was enough for Sojourner! She stood up.
She *stepped* from the back of that church to the front.
She *stormed* past the stupidity of the men who had
just spoken.

Sojourner put one big-black-beautiful foot in front of
the other and she *stomped* on the floorboards of ignorance
that were underneath. To her, the arguments made by the
men were the beetles from her past. She couldn't wait to
stomp-stomp-stomp all over them.

Sojourner took each man's belief and slammed it down like a nail. Her fist struck a hammer's blow to the podium. *Bam!*

She said, "You say women need to be helped into carriages and lifted over ditches. Nobody ever helps me into carriages. And ain't I a woman?" *Bam!*

Down came Sojourner's hand. An iron fist, smashing the lies of the day. *Bam! Bam!*

"Look at me!" Sojourner went on. "I have plowed. And I have planted. And I have gathered into barns. No man could head me. And ain't *I* a woman?"

Now Sojourner was ready to preach her beliefs about what the Bible meant to her. She spoke to the man who told of God's will. "Where did *your* Christ come from?" she asked. "From God and a woman. Man had nothing to do with Him!"

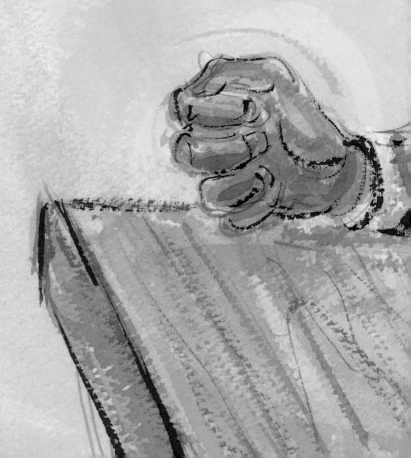

Then Sojourner talked about Eve and the apple in the Garden of Eden. She said, "If the first woman God ever made was strong enough to turn the world upside down, all alone," then women "ought to be able to turn it back and get it right side up again."

Down came both fists. *Bam! Bam!*

When Sojourner was done, she told the congregation, "Now old Sojourner hasn't got nothing more to say."

And that was the truth! Sojourner had spoken the honest-to-goodness. She was ready to step. And step she did. Her size-twelves hit their stride. Off she walked.

Big. Black. Beautiful. True.
That was Sojourner.

More about Sojourner Truth

Sojourner Truth was born in Ulster County, New York, in 1797. The exact date is unknown. She was the ninth child born to her parents.

Even as a girl, Sojourner had a deep belief in God. She often felt "led" by God's guidance. This prompted her to take the name Sojourner Truth.

Sojourner Truth was the mother of five children. She often fled with them in tow. Over the course of her lifetime she managed to obtain freedom for them all.

After Sojourner's book was published, she supported herself with its proceeds. The book had an introduction by noted abolitionist William Lloyd Garrison.

Sojourner's shawl, bonnet and, in later life, her wire-rimmed glasses became her signature dress. This clothing was similar to Quaker attire.

By the early 1850s, Sojourner had become a popular lecturer in many states. Posters announced her upcoming engagements. She spoke to standing-room-only crowds. She often sang hymns during her speeches.

A women's abolitionist group made Sojourner a white banner that said: "Proclaim liberty throughout the land and to all the inhabitants thereof." She sometimes wore this for public appearances.

As she traveled, Sojourner kept a "Book of Life"—a scrapbook of mementos. On October 29, 1864, Sojourner met President Abraham Lincoln, who signed her book: "For Aunty Sojourner Truth."

Sojourner Truth died on November 26, 1883, in Battle Creek, Michigan. She was about eighty-six. Her friend Olive Gilbert visited two weeks before her death. Sojourner sang this hymn to Olive on that day:

It was early in the morning,
It was early in the morning,
Just at the break of day,
When He rose, when He rose,
    when He rose,
And went to heaven on a cloud.

For Further Reading

Frazier, Thomas R., ed. *Afro-American History: Primary Sources.* New York: Harcourt Brace Jovanovich, 1970.

Hine, Darlene Clark, ed. *Black Women in America: An Historical Encyclopedia. Vol. 2 M–Z.* Brooklyn: Carlson Publishing, 1993.

Krass, Peter. *Sojourner Truth.* Black Americans of Achievement Series. New York: Chelsea House Publishers, 1988.

McKissack, Patricia C., and Frederick McKissack. *Sojourner Truth—Ain't I a Woman?* New York: Scholastic, 1992.

Redding, J. Saunders. "Sojourner Truth" in *Notable American Women 1607–1950 Volume III P–Z.* Edward T. James, editor. Janet Wilson James and Paul S. Boyer, assistant editors. Cambridge, Massachusetts: Belknap Press, 1971.

Truth, Sojourner. *Narrative of Sojourner Truth.* Nell Irvin Painter, contributor. New York: Penguin Classics, 1998.

For Susie—A.D.P.

To my mother, Gloria,
and her step-stomp stride—B.P.

This book is set in Opti Packard.
Designed by Judythe Sieck & Scott Piehl

Printed in Singapore

Reinforced binding
Library of Congress Cataloging-in-Publication Data on file.
ISBN 978-0-7868-0767-3
Visit www.hyperionbooksforchildren.com